CLOUD NINE

For Tony and Elizabeth — J.O.

Clarion Books
a Houghton Mifflin Company imprint
215 Park Avenue South, New York, NY 10003
Text copyright © 1995 by Norman Silver
Illustrations copyright © 1995 by Jan Ormerod

First published in the United Kingdom 1995
by The Bodley Head Children's Books
Random House, 20 Vauxhall Bridge Road, London SW1V 2SA

For information about permission to reproduce selections from
this book, write to Permissions, Houghton Mifflin Company,
215 Park Avenue South, New York, NY 10003.

Printed in Hong Kong

10 9 8 7 6 5 4 3 2 1

Library of Congress Cataloging-in-Publication Data

Silver, Norman.
    Cloud nine / Norman Silver; illustrated by Jan Ormerod.
        p. cm.
Summary: It's much too noisy at Armstrong's house, so when
his dad tells him to go outside, Armstrong builds himself a
ladder up to the clouds where he can have some peace and quiet.
    ISBN 0-395-73545-9
    [1. Noise—Fiction. 2. Clouds—Fiction. 3. Family life—
Fiction.] I. Ormerod, Jan, ill. II. Title.
PZ 7.S585736C1 1995
[E]—dc20   94-43853
                                                CIP
                                                AC

Norman Silver
CLOUD NINE
Illustrated by Jan Ormerod

Clarion Books
New York

Armstrong's house was noisy.

His mom was vacuuming the living-room carpet. The TV was on loud, and so was Bubbles. (Bubbles was his younger sister.) His dad was shouting at Chum, the puppy, for chewing the table leg. And Chum was barking, "HRRIFF-HRRUFF!"

"Silly child!" his mother said to Armstrong, as a piece of plastic brick got sucked into the vacuum cleaner. "That's not a good place to play."

"Silly chide!" Bubbles said, as she hammered her toy xylophone.

"Silly child!" his dad said, as he tripped over the moonbase Armstrong was building. "Go outside and build!"

"*HRRIFF-HRRUFF!*" Chum barked.

Armstrong went outside. He took a hammer, screwdriver, saw, wrench, nails, screws, nuts, bolts, and rope, and set to work. Using planks and poles, he built a ladder on the patch of grass in the backyard.

The ladder grew higher and higher. Higher than the fence, higher than the shed, higher than the house – into the blue sky, one rung at a time.

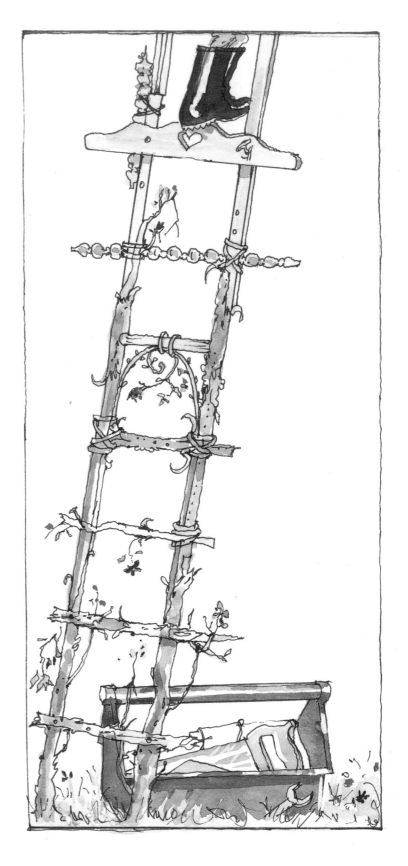

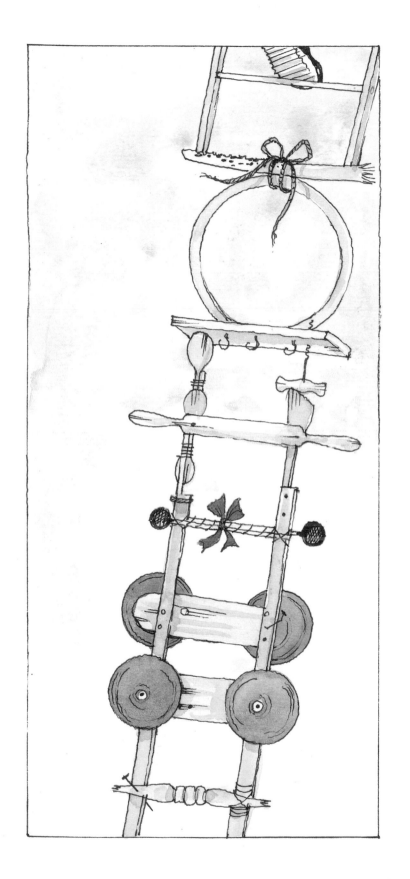

Soon the ladder was as high as the clouds. He watched eight clouds sail by, slowly and silently.

Then, using a rope, he captured the next cloud and tied it to the ladder. Armstrong climbed up on it.

"I'm the first boy on a cloud," he said.

The cloud was more bouncy than his mom and dad's mattress.

Armstrong trampolined and jumped and somersaulted and skipped and rolled around on the cloud.

The cloud had interesting caves to hide in – soft, secret places that no one had ever been in before. Places to curl up in and have a rest.

And it was so quiet! If he listened hard, he could only just hear his dad clanking the pots and pans and his mom mowing the lawn and Bubbles yelling and Chum barking.

If he looked over the edge, he could see his ladder stretching all the way down to the tiny patch of grass in his tiny backyard.

"My house is so small," he said, "only an ant family could live in it."

He could see ant-mom mowing the lawn, and ant-sister riding her tricycle, and ant-dad washing the car, and ant-dog chasing around in circles.

He could see that his house was part of a town. The town was part of a countryside. And the countryside stretched all the way to the high mountain peaks in the distance. Above him, the sun shone the brightest yellow in the clearest, bluest sky he had ever seen.

Suddenly Armstrong heard a voice behind him. It was the mailman. He had climbed up the ladder with a heavy sack of letters over his shoulder. He gave Armstrong a letter.

It read:

Dear Armstrong,

We miss you.
Please come home.

Love from Mom,
Dad, Bubbles,
and Chum.

"I don't miss them very much," said Armstrong to the mailman. "They're a noisy bunch!"

The mailman asked if he could climb onto the cloud.

"No! This is Cloud 9. Go find your own!"

Armstrong cut the rope that tied his cloud to the ladder.

The cloud floated away, leaving the mailman perched in midair.

When Armstrong looked down, he saw the town becoming smaller and smaller as he drifted far from it. He couldn't hear his mom singing. Or his dad playing the stereo. Or Bubbles banging on the cardboard box. Or Chum whining.

Armstrong lay on his cloud, enjoying the quiet blue sky.

Above him, he heard the noise of an engine. It was an airplane. The pilot, wearing goggles, called down to him, "Can you possibly be Armstrong, the first boy on a cloud?"

"I am," said Armstrong, "and I don't want to go home."

"Your mom and dad are missing you," the pilot said.

"Well, I'm not missing them," Armstrong said.

A strong wind carried Cloud 9 through the sky.

"Wouldn't it be fun," Armstrong said, "if I could steer this cloud toward the mountains?"

He took off his shirt and used it as a sail. The cloud changed direction and Armstrong steered it toward the mountain peaks.

It was beautiful sailing between the mountains.

Until he heard a mountaineer calling to him, "Excuse me, young man, are you by any chance called Armstrong?"

"I am," Armstrong said, "and I don't miss my mom and dad."

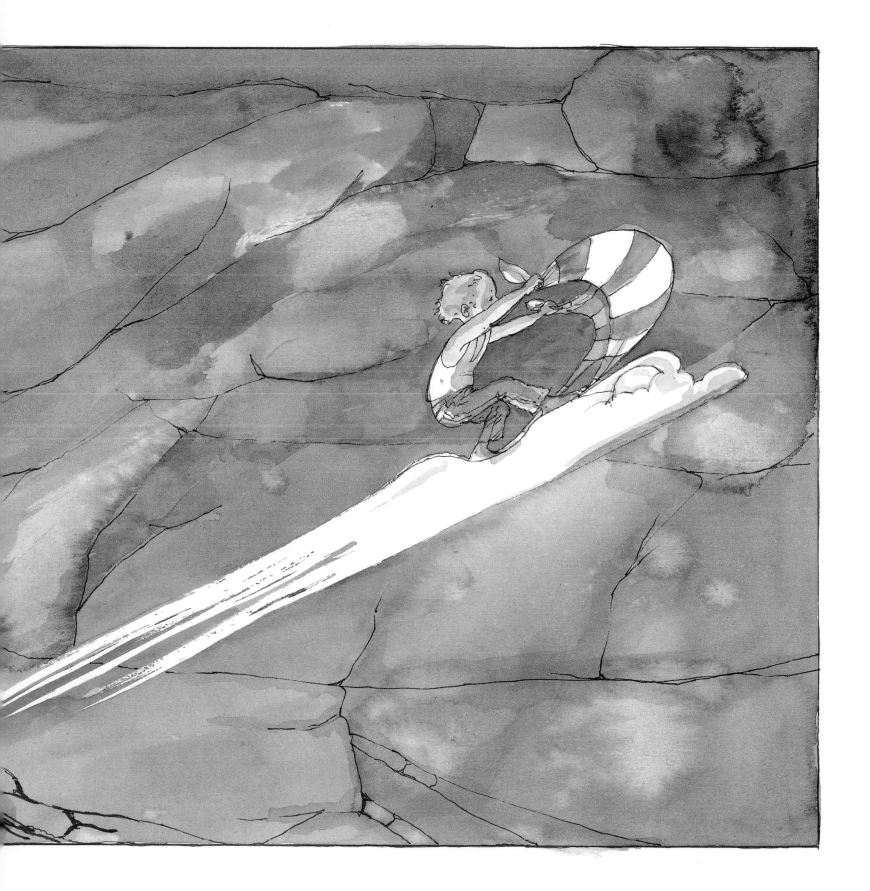

Just then a fierce gust blew the cloud too close to the enormous peaks. Armstrong knew it was dangerous.

"This cloud is going to bump," he said, "unless I steer carefully."

Using the sail, he tried to steer away from the sharp, pointed peaks, but

ZZZZRRRRIPPPP!!!

the cloud struck one of them.

Cloud 9 had sprung a leak! Air and drops of water gushed out of the hole.

Armstrong held on tightly as his cloud whooshed through the sky like a deflating balloon, raining on everything below.

The more it leaked, the lower it sank, shrinking smaller and smaller. He sat on it, shouting, "*YIPPEEEE!*" as it flew above the trees, soaking them with its drizzle.

"This cloud is going to crash!" Armstrong said.

He was right.

It crash-landed in a field of long grass.

Armstrong saw his mom and dad and Bubbles and Chum running across the field toward him. They were soaked through.

"Are you all right?" Dad asked.

"We missed you," Mom said.

"Silly chide!" said Bubbles.

As soon as they were back inside the house, his dad switched on the stereo, his mom started talking on the phone, and Bubbles started yelling. Chum licked Armstrong all over and yapped with pleasure, *"HRRIFF-HRRUFF!"*

"It was much too quiet on Cloud 9," Armstrong said, as he went to hang the cloud over the end of his bed.